JUDY MOODY AND FRIENDS

Frank Pearl in
The Awful Waffle Kerfuffle

Megan McDonald

illustrated by Erwin Madrid
based on the characters
created by Peter H. Reynolds

CANDLEWICK PRESS

For Richard

M. M.

For my nieces, Melanie and Mariel

E. M.

Text copyright © 2014 by Megan McDonald
Illustrations copyright © 2014 by Peter H. Reynolds
Judy Moody font copyright © 2003 by Peter H. Reynolds
Judy Moody®. Judy Moody is a registered trademark of Candlewick Press, Inc.

First edition 2014

Library of Congress Catalog Card Number 2013952831
ISBN 978-0-7636-5717-8 (hardcover)
ISBN 978-0-7636-7213-3 (paperback)

14 15 16 17 18 19 CCP 10 9 8 7 6 5 4 3 2 1

Printed in Shenzhen, Guangdong, China

This book was typeset in ITC Stone Informal.
The illustrations were created digitally.

Candlewick Press
99 Dover Street
Somerville, Massachusetts 02144

visit us at www.candlewick.com

CONTENTS

CHAPTER 1
The Fro-Yo Yo-Yo Contest

Frank Pearl walked the dog down Jumper Street. He walked the dog down Croaker Road. He walked the dog past Judy Moody's house.

"What's up, Frank?" Judy called.

"I'm walking the dog," said Frank.

"But there's no dog," said Judy. "How can you walk the dog without a dog?"

Frank held up his brand-new, super-sleek Whizz Master 5000 yo-yo. It was Fast with a capital *F*. "Walking the Dog is a yo-yo trick."

"When you're done walking your yo-yo," Judy asked, "want to go look for turtles?"

"Can't. I have to Rock the Baby," said Frank.

"Baby? What baby?"

"Then I have to Skin the Cat."

"More yo-yo tricks?" said Judy.

Frank nodded. "I'm on my way to the frozen-yogurt shop. Today is the Fro-Yo Yo-Yo contest."

"Whoa-whoa. Wait a minute. You hate contests."

"I hate *not winning* contests," said Frank. "Just once I want to be the best-ever, blue-ribbon, one-of-a-kind winner at something."

Frank walked the dog all the way to Fro-Yo World, with Judy right beside him.

Swoosh! Whoosh! Doing! Boing! Fro-Yo World was full of Atom Smashers. It was full of Flying Saucers. It was full of Time Warps and Tidal Waves.

"Ricky Ricasa!" said Frank, pointing.

"No way!" said Judy. "Who's Ricky Ricasa?"

"Mr. Whizz Master himself. Fastest Flying Trapeze in the East."

"Rare!" said Judy.

"He's going to show us his famous tricks before the contest. The kid with the best yo-yo trick gets to name a fro-yo flavor."

Just then, Ricky Ricasa got out his Super Deluxe Titanium Series 3 Orbiter.

It gleamed. It glistened. It glinted in the light.

Swish! Swash! Whizzzz! That yo-yo popped up off the ground. That yo-yo flew through the air. That yo-yo spun and swung and twisted and looped.

Brain Twister!

Eiffel Tower!

Punching Bag!

When the show was over, the crowd
went wild.

"Warm up those yo-yos," said Ricky
Ricasa. "Gimme what you got."

A kid with red hair went
Around the World.

A girl with ponytails
Walked the Tightrope.

A guy with a frog voice
showed off a Shooting Star.

8

Then Paisley Parker did the Boingy Boing—with sound effects! The Boingy Boing was Expert Level Three. She started with a Split Bottom Mount. Then she bounced and boinged that yo-yo back and forth more than sixteen times!

WHOOSH!

At last it was Frank's turn. "My trick is called the Flying Skunk. It's a cross between the Shooting Star and the Flying Saucer."

Frank let his yo-yo drop to the floor. He wound the string around and around. He pulled back and *WHAMMO*. His yo-yo hung in the air for one, two, three seconds, spinning madly. Lights blinked and flashed like fireworks.

That skunk was flying!

At last, Frank flicked his finger to call that skunk home. But the yo-yo spun out of orbit. It zigged. It zagged. That yo-yo went cuckoo!

"Duck!" Judy yelled.

Yikes! The runaway string wrapped around Frank's head. The string looped over his ear. The string tangled up in his glasses. Frank's glasses crashed to the floor. *Smasheroo!*

He put them back on. The blinking yo-yo still dangled from his glasses. The crowd roared.

"Looks like this young man got skunked," Ricky Ricasa teased. "Good trick. Keep working on that landing."

Frank plopped beside Judy. "The skunk stunk," said Frank. "*And* I broke my glasses."

"You could still win," said Judy.

"Drumroll, please," said Ricky Ricasa. "And the winner is . . . everybody! Line up for your *free* mini fro-yo."

"But who gets to name that fro-yo flavor?" asked Frank.

"That would be Paisley Parker for the Boingy Boing!" Everybody clapped.

"Oh, man! I wanted to name that yogurt the Flying Skunk," Frank told Judy.

"Skunk fro-yo? P.U." said Judy.

Frank stepped up to get his free mini cone. It sure was mini. "They should name this Thumbelina," said Frank.

Paisley Parker was holding a not-mini, double-decker, triple-swirl fro-yo. It was drip-drip-drippy.

"Your trick was awesome," said Frank. "And your dismount? Wow. It was like a yo-yo somersault."

"Thanks," said Paisley. Her fro-yo dripped all over the floor.

"Don't you like your fro-yo?" Judy asked.

"I'm allergic," said Paisley. "But I still have to think up a name for it."

"I'll help," said Frank. He took a lick. He took another lick. Lick-lick-lick-lick-lick.

"Any ideas?" asked Paisley.

"Don't say Flying Skunk," said Judy.

"I'd call this the . . . Yo-Yoing,
Double-Boing, Banana-Split-
Destroying Somersault." *Slurp!*

CHAPTER 2
The Kooky Cookie Contest

"Guess what," Frank told Judy. "I'm going to enter Cookie in a contest."

"A cookie contest?" said Judy. "Let's make snickerdoodles!"

"Snickerdoodle," said Cookie the parrot.

"No, I'm going to enter Cookie, *my parrot,* in a contest."

"What about yo-yos?" Judy asked.

"I was a yo-yo to think I could win a yo-yo contest," said Frank.

"Frank's a yo-yo," said Cookie.

"Am not!" said Frank.

"Frank eats paste," said Cookie.

"My sister taught her *that* one," said Frank.

"Beddy-bye. Nighty-night," said Cookie.

"It's not bedtime," said Frank. "Time to learn a new trick."

"What tricks can she do?" Judy asked.

"She can hang upside down. She can waddle her butt to music. And when she hears the vacuum cleaner, she says, 'Frank's a poopy head.'"

"Funny! Do that one," said Judy.

"The contest is called Pets Are Family. Cookie's trick has to show that she's a special part of my family."

Cookie hopped onto Frank's arm. Frank held out a peanut.

"Gimme kiss," said Frank.

"Waak!" Cookie ruffled her feathers.

"Gimme kiss," said Frank.

"Waak!" Cookie bobbed her head up and down.

"Cookie. You can do this," said Frank. "Gimme kiss."

"Waak! Gimme kiss," said Cookie. *"Mww! Mww! Mww!"*

Judy clapped. "She did it! She even made funny smooching sounds."

"Good girl," said Frank. He gave her a peanut.

"Good girl," said Cookie.

On the day of the contest, Judy and Rocky met Frank at Fur & Fangs.

"There's a parrot here named Rocky!" said Rocky.

"Dirty bird. Dirty bird," said Cookie.

"What's the prize, anyway?" asked Rocky.

"Who cares?" said Frank. "Just once I want to win a contest like you guys!"

"What did I ever win?" asked Rocky.

"You won a trick deck of cards at the House of Magic."

"I'm a pirate," said Cookie. "Cap'n Cookie."

"Stop that," said Frank.

"Stop that," said Cookie.

Frank frowned at his parrot. "And Judy won a famous pet contest," he said.

"My *cat* won," said Judy.

"You still got your picture in the paper," Frank said.

Judy held up her elbow. "I got my *elbow* in the paper."

"Welcome to Pets Are Family Day!" said Mrs. Birdwistle, the pet store lady. "And a warm welcome to our furry and feathered friends!"

"Frank eats paste," said Cookie.
Everybody cracked up.

Luna, a cat wearing
glasses, pretended to
read.

A guinea pig named
Dorothy played
Scrabble. She nudged
the letters *P-I-G* with her nose!

There was even a
dog named Bo who
could take out the
trash.

Everybody clapped. Bo got so excited that he knocked over the trash can!

"Sorry about that," said his owner.

"No worries," said Mrs. Birdwistle. "We'll get this cleaned up in no time."

At last it was Cookie's turn.

"Dirty bird!" said Cookie. "Dirty bird!"

Cookie perched on Frank's arm. "Hi. My name is Frank Pearl and this is Cookie. Our trick is called Gimme Kiss."

Frank held out a peanut. "Ready? Gimme kiss."

"Lu, lu, lu, lu," said Cookie.

"Not lulu," said Frank. "C'mon,
Cookie. You can do this. Gimme kiss."

RrrooaaRR! Vacuum cleaner!
Somebody turned on the vacuum to
clean up the trash.

"Frank is a poopy head!" sang Cookie. She raced up and down Frank's arm. "Poopy head!" Cookie hopped up onto Frank's head, flapping her wings wildly. "Frank is a big sister." The crowd went crazy.

"The vacuum freaks her out," said
Frank. He rushed Cookie out the door.
Judy and Rocky ran after him.

"*You're* a poopy head," Frank said to Cookie.

"It wasn't her fault," said Judy. "It was the vacuum cleaner."

"There goes another contest down the tubes."

"Down the tubes!" said Cookie.

"Cookie, don't you get it?" Frank asked. "I'm mad at you. Don't say a word. Not one more word."

Cookie ruffled her feathers. Cookie bobbed her head. Cookie wiggled her butt.

"Gimme kiss!" said Cookie. *"Mww! Mww! Mww!"*

CHAPTER 3
The Awful Waffle Kerfuffle

Frank pointed to the poster in the school lunchroom. His mouth fell open. A glob of ABC sandwich fell out.

"Gross!" said Judy Moody and Jessica Finch.

"Gross!" said Amy and Rocky.

THE GREAT THIRD-GRADE BREAKFAST BASH AND WAFFLE-OFF!

This Saturday in the school cafeteria

• Families welcome •
• Prizes for best waffles •
• Proceeds go to third-grade field trip •

"Look! It's the Great Third-Grade Breakfast Bash! We get to come to the cafeteria on Saturday with our families and eat breakfast."

"What's so great about breakfast?" asked Rocky.

"It's only the most important meal of the day," Jessica Finch said.

"Breakfast tastes like pencil shavings," said Rocky.

"But this year it's a Waffle-Off," said Frank. "To raise money for our third-grade field trip."

"So we can go to the Smelly Jelly Bean factory!" said Judy. "Where they make weird flavors of jelly beans, like toothpaste and rotten eggs."

"What's a Waffle-Off?" asked Amy.

"The Waffle-Off is the best contest *ever*," said Frank. "It's to see who can make the best, most amazing waffle."

"They give out blue ribbons for all kinds of waffles," said Jessica. "Like Most Blueberries, Whipped Creamiest, and Best Use of Sprinkles."

"I'm going to win," said Frank. "I can feel it!"

"Are you off your waffle, Frank?" asked Judy.

"You can't even cook," Rocky said. "Can you?"

"Parents make the waffles," Jessica told them. "All you have to do is dress up your waffle fancy with whipped cream and sprinkles and stuff. Then Mr. Todd gives out ribbons before they get eaten."

Frank and his friends got quiet, dreaming about waffles.

"I've got a great idea for my waffle!" said Frank.

"Is your waffle a *sandwich*?" Judy asked. "Mine is going to be a whipped-cream sandwich."

"Does your waffle play sports?" Rocky asked. "Mine is going to play sports. And it's not going to taste like pencil shavings."

"My idea snap-crackle-pops! My idea will *blow* your mind. It's all about the *fizz*-i-cality. Just you wait."

At last it was Saturday. "Welcome to the Great Third-Grade Breakfast Bash," said Mr. Todd. "Thanks for coming to our Waffle-Off! I hope you're all ready to *break an egg*." Everybody laughed.

"Ready, set, waffle!" Moms and dads poured batter onto sizzling waffle irons. *Pssh!* Fluffy, puffy golden waffles!

Judy's waffle sandwich was held up
with pizza tables.

Rocky's waffle looked like a soccer ball.

Amy's waffle had her name spelled in blueberries.

Then came the Piggy on a Pillow, made by Jessica A. Finch. A puffy pink cloud of whipped cream floated on top of her waffle. It was sprinkled with sugar glitter. On top was a sugar-dusted candy piggy with rosy-red cheeks.

"I can win for the pinkest or prettiest waffle," said Jessica.

"Or piggiest," Judy teased.

Frank had hidden his top-secret, none-of-your-beeswax waffle under a cake dome. "Ta da!" said Frank. "Presenting"—he lifted the lid—"the Super-Amazing Exploding Volcano Waffle!" A hill, a mountain, a tower of brown jelly beans rose up from that waffle like a volcano. The Mount Vesuvius of all waffles.

Marshmallow Fluff spewed from a hole in the top. *Pop, pop, fizz, fizz.* Fizzlers, wizzlers, and sizzlers popped and exploded like lava.

"Wait till Mr. Todd sees this!" said Frank. "Blue ribbon, here I come!"

Then, all of a sudden, the fizzlers fizzled and the wizzlers melted into the sizzlers. Rainbow-colored lava oozed down the jelly-bean mountain. *Plop!* The glop hit the floor in one giant gluppy glob of gloop.

"OOH! Gross! Bluck!" said all the kids.

"Mount Vesuvius meltdown!" said Frank.

Stink came running over to see.

"What's all this waffle kerfuffle?" asked Mr. Todd.

"It's Frank's Super-Amazing Exploding Waffle," said Judy.

"Super-Amazing *Disaster* Waffle," said Frank. "It was supposed to be an exploding volcano. But the jelly beans caved in. And all the Pop Rocks ran together. Now it just looks like a giant mud pie."

He ran to grab a towel from the kitchen. On his way, he passed the prize table full of ribbons. Shiny blue ribbons that called out MOST! BEST! BIGGEST! FANCIEST! He would never win the contest now. He would no-way no-how be taking home a ribbon.

When he came back with the towel, Frank could not believe his eyes. There, gleaming in a beam of sunlight, was none other than one of those very same big shiny blue prize ribbons. The ribbon was on *his waffle*. The Mount Vesuvius Meltdown.

Stink yelled and pointed. "Hey, Frank! You won! You won the awful waffle contest!"

"But *not* for being awful," said Judy.

Frank leaned in and read the ribbon. ONE OF A KIND! "I won? I actually won a contest? With a real blue ribbon?" He looked at Mr. Todd.

"Your waffle is in a class by itself, Frank."

Frank stuck the blue ribbon on his shirt and grinned.

"It's one of a kind," said Mr. Todd. "Just like you."

Stink chewed on a jelly bean from Frank's waffle. "Hey!" He made a face. "It tastes like pencil shavings."

"Told you!" said Rocky.

"I like it! Got any more?"

Frank laughed. "Ha, ha. Those are Smelly Jelly jelly beans. They *look* like maple syrup, but the flavor is pencil shavings."

"Clever," said Mr. Todd. "I like how you tied it into our class field trip to the Smelly Jelly Bean factory."

"Too bad you don't win *money* with that ribbon," said Rocky. "Then you could buy more Smelly jellies."

Stink reached into his pocket. He pulled out a dollar bill. "One dollar! I'll give you one whole dollar bill for the one-of-a-kindest, awfulest, most delicious waffle in the world!"

"Sold!" said Frank.